Richard Le Gallienne

English Poems

Richard Le Gallienne

English Poems

ISBN/EAN: 9783337158125

Printed in Europe, USA, Canada, Australia, Japan

Cover: Foto ©Andreas Hilbeck / pixelio.de

More available books at **www.hansebooks.com**

Of this edition Eight hundred copies have been printed for England and America

English Poems

By Richard Le-Gallienne.

A.D. 1892.

London: Elkin Mathews and John Lane at The Bodley Head. New York: The Cassell Publishing Company, 104, Fourth Aven℮.

To Sissie Le Gallienne

a 2

EPISTLE DEDICATORY

Dear Sister: Hear the conclusion of the whole matter. You dream like mad, you love like tinder, you aspire like a star-struck moth—for what? That you may hive little lyrics, and sell to a publisher for thirty pieces of silver.

Hard by us here is a ' bee-farm.' It always reminds me of a publisher's. The bee has loved a thousand flowers, through a hundred afternoons, he has filled little sacred cells with the gold of his stolen kisses—for what? That the whole should be wrenched away and sold at so much ' the comb'—as though it were a hair-comb. 'Mummy is become merchandise . . . and Pharaoh is sold for balsams.'

Can we ever forget those old mornings when we rose with the lark, and, while the earliest sunlight slanted through the sleeping house, stole to the little viii   EPISTLE DEDICATORY

bookclad study to read—Heaven bless us !—you, perhaps, Mary Wollstonecraft, and I, Livy, in a Froben folio of 1531.

Will you accept these old verses in memory of those old mornings ? Ah, then came in the sweet o' the year.

Yours now as then,

R. Le G.

May 14th, 1892.

CONTENTS

x CONTENTS

CONTENTS

ENGLISH POEMS

A

TO THE READER

Art was a palace once, things great and fair,
And strong and holy, found a temple there :
Now 'tis a lazar-house of leprous men.
O shall we hear an English song again !
Still English larks mount in the merry morn,
An English May still brings an English thorn,
Still English daisies up and down the grass,
Still English love for English lad and lass—
Yet youngsters blush to sing an English song !

Thou nightingale that for six hundred years
Sang to the world—O art thou husht at last !
For, not of thee this new voice in our ears,
Music of France that once was of the spheres ;
And not of thee these strange green flowers that
    spring
From daisy roots and seem to bear a sting.

Thou Helicon of numbers ' undefiled,'
Forgive that 'neath the shadow of thy name,
England, I bring a song of little fame ;
Not as one worthy but as loving thee,
Not as a singer, only as a child.

PAOLO AND FRANCESCA

To R. K. Leather

(July 16th, 1892.)

PAOLO AND FRANCESCA

It happened in that great Italian land
    Where every bosom beateth with a star—
At Rimini, anigh that crumbling strand
    The Adriatic filcheth near and far—
      In that same past where Dante's dream-days are,
That one Francesca gave her youthful gold
    Unto an aged carle to bolt and bar;
Though all the love which great young hearts
      can hold,
How could she give that love unto a miser old?

Nay! but young Paolo was the happy lad,
    A youth of dreaming eye yet dauntless foot,
Who all Francesca's wealth of loving had;
    One brave to scale a wall and steal the fruit,
      Nor fear because some dotard owned the root;
Yea! one who wore his love like sword on thigh
    And kept not all his valour for his lute;
One who could dare as well as sing and sigh.
Ah! then were hearts to love, but they are long
    gone by.

Ye lily-wives so happy in the nest,
   Whose joy within the gates of duty springs,
Blame not Love's poor, who, if they would be blest,
   Must steal what comes to you with marriage
      rings:
   Ye pity the poor lark whose scarce-tried wings
Faint in the net, while still the morning air
   With brown free throats of all his brethren sings,
And can it be ye will not pity her,
Whose youth is as a lark all lost to singing there.

In opportunity of dear-bought joy
   Rich were this twain, for old Lanciotto, he
Who was her lord, was brother of her boy,
   And in one home together dwelt the three,
   With brothers two beside; and he and she
Sat at one board together, in one fane
   Their voices rose upon one hymn, ah me!
Beneath one roof each night their limbs were
      lain,
As now in death they share the one eternal pain.

As much as common men can love a flower
   Unto Lanciotto was Francesca dear,
'Tis not on such Love wields his jealous power;
   And therefore Paolo moved him not to fear,

Though he so green with youth and he so sere.
Nor yet indeed was wrong, the hidden thing
    Grew at each heart, unknown of each, a year,—
Two eggs still silent in the nest through spring,
May draws so near to June, and not yet time to sing!

    Yet oft, indeed, through days that gave no sign
        Had but Francesca turned about and read
Paolo's bright eyes that only dared to shine
        On the dear gold that glorified her head ;
        Ere all the light had from their circles fled
And the grey Honour darkened all his face :
        They had not come to June and nothing said,
Day followed day with such an even pace,
Nor night succeeded night and left no starry trace.

    Or, surely, had the flower Paolo pressed
        In some sweet volume when he put it by,
Told how his mistress drew it to her breast
        And called upon his name when none was nigh ;
        Had but the scarf he kissed with piteous cry
But breathed again its secret unto her,
        Or had but one of every little sigh
Each left for each been love's true messenger :
They surely had not kept that winter all the year.

Yea ! love lay hushed and waiting like a seed,
    Some laggard of the season still abed
Though the sun calls and gentle zephyrs plead,
    And Hope that waited long must deem it dead ;
    Yet lo ! to-morrow sees its shining head
Singing at dawn 'mid all the garden throng :
    Ah, had it known, it had been earlier sped—
Was it for fear of day it slept so long,
Or were its dreams of singing sweeter than the song?

But what poor flower can symbol all the might
    And all the magnitude, great Love, of thee ?
Ah, is there aught can image thee aright
    In earth or heaven, how great or fair it be ?
    We watch the acorn grow into the tree,
We watch the patient spark surprise the mine,
    But what are oaks to thy Ygdrasil-tree ?
What the mad mine's convulsive strength to thine,
That wrecks a world but bids heaven's soaring
    steeples shine.

A god that hath no earthly metaphor,
    A blinding word that hath no earthly rhyme,
Love ! we can only call and no name more ;
    As the great lonely thunder rolls sublime,
    As the great sun doth solitary climb,

And we have but themselves to know them by,
　　Just so Love stands a stranger amid Time :
The god is there, the great voice speaks on high,
We pray, 'What art thou, Lord ?' but win us no reply.

So in the dark grew Love, but feared to flower,
　　Dreamed to himself, but never spake a word,
Burned like a prisoned fire from hour to hour,
　　Sang his dear song like an unheeded bird ;
　　Waiting the summoning voice so long unheard,
Waiting with weary eyes the gracious sign
　　To bring his rose, and tell the dream he dared,
The tremulous moment when the star should shine,
And each should ask of each, and each should answer
　　—'Thine.'

Winter to-day, but lo ! to-morrow spring !
　　They waited long, but O at last it came,
Came in a silver hush at evening ;
　　Francesca toyed with threads upon a frame,
　　Hard by young Paolo read of knight and dame
That long ago had loved and passed away :
　　He had no other way to tell his flame,
She dare not listen any other way—
But even that was bliss to lovers poor as they.

The world grew sweet with wonder in the west
　　The while he read and while she listened there,

And many a dream from out its silken nest
   Stole like a curling incense through the air ;
   Yet looked she not on him, nor did he dare :
But when the lovers kissed in Paradise
   His voice sank and he turned his gaze on her,
Like a young bird that flutters ere it flies,—
And lo ! a shining angel called him from her eyes.

Then from the silence sprang a kiss like flame,
   And they hung lost together ; while around
The world was changed, no more to be the same
   Meadow or sky, no little flower or sound
Again the same, for earth grew holy ground :
While in the silence of the mounting moon
   Infinite love throbbed in the straining bound
Of that great kiss, the long-delaying boon,
Granted indeed at last, but ended, ah ! so soon.

As the great sobbing fulness of the sea
   Fills to the throat some void and aching cave,
Till all its hollows tremble silently,
   Pressed with sweet weight of softly-lapping
      wave :
So kissed those mighty lovers glad and brave.
And as a sky from which the sun has gone
   Trembles all night with all the stars he gave—

A firmament of memories of the sun,—
So thrilled and thrilled each life when that great
  kiss was done.

But coward shame that had no word to say
    In passion's hour, with sudden icy clang
Slew the bright morn, and through the tarnished
    day
      An iron bell from light to darkness rang :
      She shut her ears because a throstle sang,
    She dare not hear the little innocent bird,
      And a white flower made her poor head to hang—
    To be so white ! once she was white as curd,
But now—'Alack !' 'Alack !' She speaks no other
    word.

The pearly line on yonder hills afar
    Within the dawn, when mounts the lark and
      sings
By the great angel of the morning star,—
      That was his love, and all free fair fresh things
      That move and glitter while the daylight springs :
    To thus know love, and yet to spoil love thus !
      To lose the dream—O silly beating wings—
    Great dream so splendid and miraculous :
O Lord, O Lord, have mercy, have mercy upon us.

She turned her mind upon the holy ones
  Whose love lost here was love in heaven tenfold,
She thought of Lucy, that most blessed of nuns
  Who sent her blue eyes on a plate of gold
  To him who wooed her daily for her love—
'Mine eyes!' 'Mine eyes!' 'Here,—go in peace,
    they are!'
  But ever love came through the midnight grove,
Young Love, with wild eyes watching from afar,
And called and called and called until the morning
    star.

Ah, poor Francesca, 'tis not such as thou
  That up the stony steeps of heaven climb;
Take thou thy heaven with thy Paolo now—
  Sweet saint of sin, saint of a deathless rhyme,
  Song shall defend thee at the bar of Time,
Dante shall set thy fair young glowing face
  On the dark background of his theme sublime,
And Thou and He in your superb disgrace
Still on that golden wind of passion shall embrace.

    .   .   .   .   .

So loved this twain, but whither have they passed?
  Ah me, that dark must always follow day,
That Love's last kiss is surely kissed at last,

Howe'er so wildly the poor lips may pray :
   Merciful God, is there no other way ?
And pen, O must thou of the ending write,
   The hour Lanciotto found them where they lay,
Folded together, weary with delight,
Within the sumptuous petals of the rose of night.

Yea, for Lanciotto found them : many an hour,
   Ere their dear joy had run its doomèd date,
Had they, in silken nook and blossomed bower,
   All unsuspect the blessed apple ate,
   Who now must grind its core predestinate.
Kiss, kiss, poor losing lovers, nor deny
   One little tremor of its bliss, for Fate
Cometh upon you, and the dark is nigh
Where all, unkissed, unkissing, learn at length to lie.

Bent on some journey of the state's concern
   They deemed him, and indeed he rode thereon :
But questioned Paolo—'What if he return !'
   'Nay, love, indeed he is securely gone
   As thou art surely here, beloved one,
He went ere sundown, and our moon is here—
   A fear, love, in this heart that yet knew none !'
How could he fright that little velvet ear
With last night's dream and all its ghostly fear !

So did he yield him to her eager breast,
   And half forgot, but could not quite forget,
No sweetest kiss could put that fear to rest,
   And all its haggard vision chilled him yet ;
   Their warder moon in nameless trouble set,
There seemed a traitor echo in the place,
   A moaning wind that moaned for lovers met,
And once above her head's deep sunk embrace
He saw—Death at the window with his yellow face.

Had that same dream caught old Lanciotto's reins,
   Bent in a weary huddle on his steed,
In darkling haste along the blindfold lanes,
   Making a clattering halt in all that speed :—
   ' Fool ! Fool !' he cried, ' O dotard fool, indeed,
So ho ! they wanton while the old man rides,'
   And on the night flashed pictures of the deed.
' Come !'—and he dug his charger's panting sides,
And all the homeward dark tore by in roaring tides.

As some great lord of acres when a thief
   Steals from his park some flower he never sees,
Calls it a lily fair beyond belief,
   Prisons the wretch, and fines before he frees ;
   Such jealous madness did Lanciotto seize :
All in an instant is Francesca dear,
   He claims the wife he never cared to please,

All in an instant seems his castle near,—
And those poor lovers sleep, forgot at last their fear.

His horse left steaming at his journey's end,
   Up through his palace stairs with springing tread
He strode ; the silence met him like a friend,
   Fain to dissuade him from that deed of dread,
   Making a breeze about his burning head,
Laying large hands of comfort on his soul ;
   Within the ashes of his cheek burned red
A long-shut rose of youth, as to the goal
Of death he sped, as once to love's own tryst he stole.

He caught a sound as of a rose's breath,
   He caught another breath of deeper lung,
Rose-leaves and oak-leaves on the wind of death ;
   He drew aside the arras where they clung
   In the dim light, so lovely and so young—
They lay in sin as in a cradle there,
   Twin babes that in one bosom nestling hung :
Even Lanciotto paused, ah, will he spare ?
Who could not quite forgive a wrong that is so fair !

The grave old clock ticked somewhere in the
     gloom,
   A dozen waiting seconds rose and fell

Ere his pale dagger flickered in the room,
  Then quenched its corpse-light in their bosoms'
    swell—
  'Thus, dears, I mate you evermore in hell.'
Their blood ran warm about them and they sighed,
  For the mad smiter did his work too well,
Just drew together softly and so died,
Fell very still and strange, and moved not side by
    side.

Yea, moved not, though two hours he watched
    the twain
  And heard their blood drip drip upon the floor,
Twice with stern voice he spake to them again,
  And then, a little tenderly, once more,—
  'Thus, dears, in hell I mate you evermore.'
And when the curious fingers of the day
  Unravelled all the dark, and morning wore,
And the young light played round them where
    they lay,
The souls were many leagues upon the hellward
    way.

LOVE PLATONIC

1

Surely at last, O Lady, the sweet moon
  That bringeth in the happy singing weather
Groweth to pearly queendom, and full soon
  Shall Love and Song go hand in hand together ;
For all the pain that all too long hath waited
  In deep dumb darkness shall have speech at last,
And the bright babe Death gave the Love he mated
  Shall leap to light and kiss the weeping past.

For all the silver morning is a-glimmer
  With gleaming spears of great Apollo's host,
And the night fadeth like a spent out swimmer
  Hurled from the headlands of some shining coast.
O, happy soul, thy mouth at last is singing,
  Drunken with wine of morning's azure deep,
Sing on, my soul, the world beneath thee swinging,
  A bough of song above a sea of sleep.

2

Who is the lady I sing ?
  Ah, how can I tell thee her praise

For whom all my life's but the string
  Of a rosary painful of days ;

Which I count with a curious smile
  As a miser who hoardeth his gain,
Though, a madhearted spendthrift the while,
  I but gather to waste again.

Yea, I pluck from the tree of the years,
  As a country maid greedy of flowers,
Each day brimming over with tears,
  And I scatter like petals its hours ;

And I trample them under my feet
  In a frenzy of cloven-hoofed swine,
And the breath of their dying is sweet,
  And the blood of their hearts is as wine.

O, I throw me low down on the ground
  And I bury my face in their death,
And only I rise at the sound
  Of a wind as it scattereth,

As it scattereth sweetly the dried
  Leaves withered and brittle and sere
Of days of old years that have died—
  And, O, it is sweet in my ear !

And I rise me and build me a pyre
   Of the whispering skeleton things,
And my heart laugheth low with the fire,
   Laugheth high with the flame as it springs ;

And above in the flickering glare
   I mark me the boughs of my tree,
My tree of the years, growing bare,
   Growing bare with the scant days to be.

Then I turn to my beads and I pray
   For the axe at the root of the tree—
Last flower, last bead—ah ! last day
   That shall part me, my darling, from thee !

And I pray for the knife on the string
   Of this rosary painful of days :
But who is the Lady I sing ?
   Ah, how can I tell thee her praise !

II

I make this rhyme of my lady and me
To give me ease of my misery,
Of my lady and me I make this rhyme
For lovers in the aftertime.
And I weave its warp from day to day
In a golden loom deep hid away

In my secret heart, where no one goes
But my lady's self, and—no one knows.

With bended head all day I pore
On a joyless task, and yet before
My eyes all day, through each weary hour,
Breathes my lady's face like a dewy flower.
Like rain it comes through the dusty air,
Like sun on the meadows to think of her;
O sweet as violets in early spring
The flower-girls to the city bring,
O, healing-bright to wintry eyes
As primrose-gold 'neath northern skies—
But O for fit thing to compare
With the joy I have in the thought of her!
So all day long doth her holy face
Bring fragrance to the barren place,
And whensoe'er it comes nearest me,
My loom it weaveth busily.

Some days there be when the loom is still
And my soul is sad as an autumn hill,
But how to tell the blessed time
When my heart is one glowing prayer of rhyme!
Think on the humming afternoon
Within some busy wood in June,
When nettle patches, drunk with the sun,

Are fiery outposts of the shade ;
While gnats keep up a dizzy reel,
And the grasshopper, perched upon his blade,
Loud drones his fairy threshing-wheel :—
Hour when some poet-wit might feign
The drowsy tune of the throbbing air
The weaving of the gossamer
In secret nooks of wood and lane—
The gossamer, silk night-robes of the flowers,
Fluttered apart by amorous morning hours.
Yea, as the weaving of the gossamer,
If truly that the mystic golden boom,
Is the strange rapture of my hidden loom,
As I sit in the light of the thought of her ;
And it weaveth, weaveth, day by day,
This parti-coloured roundelay ;
Weaving for ease of misery,
Weaving this rhyme of my lady and me,
Weaving, weaving this warp of rhyme
For lovers in the after-time.

My lady, lover, may never be mine
In the same sweet way that thine is thine,
My lady and I may never stand
By the holy altar hand in hand,
My lady and I may never rest
Through the golden midnight breast to breast,

Nor share long days of happy light
Sweet moving in each other's sight :
Yea, even must we ever miss
The honey of the chastest kiss.

III

But, Song, arise thee on a greater wing,
Nor twitter robin-like of love, nor sing
A pretty dalliance with grief—but try
Some metre like a sky,
Wherein to set
Stars that may linger yet
When I, thy master, shall have come to die.

> Twitter and tweet
>   Thy carollings
>   Of little things,
> Of fair and sweet ;
> For it is meet,
>   O robin red !
> That little theme
>   Hath little song,
>   That little head
> Hath little dream,
>   And long.

But we have starry business, such a grief
As Autumn's, dead by some forgotten sheaf,

While all the distance echoes of the wain;
Grief as an ocean's for some sudden isle
Of living green that stayed with it awhile,
   Then to oblivious deluge plunged again!
Grief as of Alps that yearn but never reach,
    Grief as of Death for Life, of Night for Day:
Such grief, O Song, how hast thou strength to
    teach,
    How hope to make assay?

IV

ONCE

Once we met, and then there came,
Like a Pentecostal flame,
    A word;
All I said not,
Only thought,
    She heard!
All I never say but sing,
Worshipping;
Wrapt in the hidden tongue
Of an ambiguous song.

How we met what need to say?
   When or where,
Years ago or yesterday,
   Here or there.

All the song is—once we met,
    She and I ;
Once, but never to forget,
    Till we die.

All the song is that we meet
    Never now—
' Hast thou yet forgotten, sweet ? '
    ' Love, hast thou ? '

v

THE DAY OF THE TWO DAFFODILS

' The daffodils are fine this year,' I said ;
' O yes, but see my crocuses,' said she.
And so we entered in and sat at talk
Within a little parlour bowered about
With garden-noises, filled with garden scent,
As some sweet sea-shell rings with pearly chimes
And sighs out fragrance of its mother's breast.

We sat at talk, and all the afternoon
Whispered about in changing silences
Of flush and sudden light and gathering shade,
As though some Maestro drew out organ stops
Somewhere in heaven.   As two within a boat

On the wide sea we sat at talk, the hours
Lapping unheeded round us as the waves.
And as such two will ofttimes pause in speech,
Gaze at high heaven and draw deep to their hearts
The infinite azure, then meet eyes again
And flash it to each other ; without words
First, and then with voice trembling as trumpets
Tremble with fierce breath, voice cadenced too
As deep as the deep sea, Æolian voice,
Voice of star-spaces, and the pine-wood's voice
In dewy mornings, Life's own awful voice :
So did we talk, gazing with God's own eyes
Into Life's deeps—ah, how they throbbed with stars !
And were we not ourselves like pulsing suns
Who, once an æon met within the void,
So fiery close, forget how far away
Each orbit sweeps, and dream a little space
Of fiery wedding.   So our hearts made answering
Lightnings all that afternoon through purple mists
Of riddled speech ; and when at last the sun,
Our sentinel, made sign beneath the trees
Of coming night, and we arose and passed
Across the threshold to the flowers again,
We knew a presence walking in the grove,
And a voice speaking through the evening's cool
Unknown before : though Love had wrought no
    wrong,

His rune was spoken, and another rhyme
Writ in his poem by the master Life.

' Pray, pluck me some,' I said.   She brought me two,
For daffodils were very fine that year,—
O very fine, but daffodils no more.

VI

WHY DID SHE MARRY HIM?

Why did she marry him?   Ah, say why!
    How was her fancy caught?
What was the dream that he drew her by,
    Or was she only bought?
Gave she her gold for a girlish whim,
    A freak of a foolish mood?
Or was it some will, like a snake in him,
    Lay a charm upon her blood?

Love of his limbs, was it that, think you?
    Body of bullock build,
Sap in the bones, and spring in the thew,
    A lusty youth unspilled?
But is it so that a maid is won,
    Such a maiden maid as she?
Her face like a lily all white in the sun,
    For such mere male as he!

Ah, why do the fields with their white and
    gold
  To Farmer Clod belong,
Who though he hath reaped and stacked and
    sold
  Hath never heard their song?
Nay, seek not an answer, comfort ye,
  The poet heard their call,
And so, dear Love, will I comfort me—
  He hath thy lease, that's all.

VII

THE LAMP AND THE STAR

Yea, let me be 'thy bachelere,'
  'Tis sweeter than thy lord;
How should I envy him, my dear,
  The lamp upon his board.
Still make his little circle bright
With boon of dear domestic light,
  While I afar,
Watching his windows in the night,
  Worship a star
For which he hath no bolt or bar.
  Yea, dear,
    Thy 'bachelere.'

VIII

ORBITS

Two stars once on their lonely way
   Met in the heavenly height,
And they dreamed a dream they might shine
     alway
   With undivided light;
Melt into one with a breathless throe,
   And beam as one in the night.

And each forgot in the dream so strange
   How desolately far
Swept on each path, for who shall change
   The orbit of a star?
Yea, all was a dream, and they still must go
   As lonely as they are.

IX

NEVER—EVER

My mouth to thy mouth
   Ah never, ah never!
My breast from thy breast
   Eternities sever;
But my soul to thy soul
   For ever and ever.

X

LOVE'S POOR

YEA, love, I know, and I would have it thus,
I know that not for us
Is springtide Passion with his fire and flowers,
I know this love of ours
Lives not, nor yet may live,
By the dear food that lips and hands can give.
Not, Love, that we in some high dream despise
The common lover's common Paradise;
Ah, God, if Thou and I
But one short hour their blessedness might try,
How could we poor ones teach
Those happy ones who half forget them rich:
For if we thus endure,
'Tis only, love, because we are so poor.

XI

COMFORT OF DANTE

DOWN where the unconquered river still flows on,
  One strong free thing within a prison's heart,
  I drew me with my sacred grief apart,
That it might look that spacious joy upon:
And as I mused, lo! Dante walked with me,
  And his face spake of the high peace of pain

Till all my grief glowed in me throbbingly
   As in some lily's heart might glow the rain.

So like a star I listened, till mine eye
   Caught that lone land across the water-way
      Wherein my lady breathed,—now breathing is—
'O Dante,' then I said, 'she more than I
   Should know thy comfort, go to *her*, I pray.'
      'Nay!' answered he, 'for she hath Beatrice.'

XII

A LOST HOUR

God gave us an hour for our tears,
One hour out of all the years,
For all the years were another's gold,
Given in a cruel troth of old.

And how did we spend his boon?
   That sweet miraculous flower
   Born to die in an hour,
Late born to die so soon.

Did we watch it with breathless breath
   By slow degrees unfold?
      Did we taste the innermost heart of it
      The honey of each sweet part of it?
   Suck all its hidden gold
To the very dregs of its death?

Nay, this is all we did with our hour—
We tore it to pieces, that precious flower;
Like any daisy, with listless mirth,
We shed its petals upon the earth;
And, children-like, when it all was done,
We cried unto God for another one.

XIII

MET ONCE MORE

O Lady, I have looked on thee once more,
Thou too hast looked on me, as thou hadst said,
And though the joy was pain, the pain was bliss,
Bliss that more happy lovers well may miss:
Captives feast richly on a little bread,
So are we very rich who are so poor.

XIV

A JUNE LILY

[*The poet dramatises his Lady's loneliness.*]

Alone! once more alone! how like a tomb
My little parlour sounds which only now
Yearned like some holy chancel with his voice.
So still! so empty! Surely one might fear
The walls should meet in ruinous collapse
That held no more his music. Yet they stand

Firm in a foolish firmness, meaningless
As frescoed sepulchre some Pharaoh built
But never came to sleep in; built, indeed,
For—that grey moth to flit in like a ghost!

Alone! another feast-day come and gone,
Watched through the weeks as in my garden there
I watch a seedling grow from blade to bud
Impatient for its blossom.   So this day
Has bloomed at last, and we have plucked its flower
And shared its sweetness, and once more the time
Is as that stalk from which but now I plucked
Its last June-lily as a parting sign.
Yea, but he seemed to love it! yet if he
But craved it in deceit of tenderness
To make my heart glow brighter with a lie!
Will it indeed be cherished as he said,
Or will he keep it near his book awhile,
And when grown rank forget it in his glass,
And leave it for the maid who dusts his room
To clear away and cast upon the heap?
Or, may be, will he bury it away
In some old drawer with other mummy-flowers?

Nay, but I wrong thee, dear one, thinking so.
My boy, my love, my poet!   Nay, I know
Thy lonely room, tomb-like to thee as mine,
Tomb-like as tomb of some returning ghost,

Seems only bright about my lily-flower.
And, mayhap, while I wrong thee thus in thought
Thou bendest o'er it, feigning for some ease
Of parted ache conceits of poet-wit
On petal and on stamen—let me try !
If lilies be alike thine is as this,
I wonder if thy reading tallies too.

Six petals with a dewdrop in their heart,
Six pure brave years, an ivory cup of tears ;
Six pearly-pillared stamens golden-crowned
Growing from out the dewdrop, and a seventh
Soaring alone trilobed and mystic green ;
Six pearl-bright years aflower with gold of joy,
Sprung from the heart of those brave tear-fed years :
But what that seventh single stamen is
My little wit must leave for thee to tell.

But neither poet nor a sibyl thou !
What brave conceit had he, my poet, built ;
No jugglery of numbers that mean nought,
That can mean nought for ever, unto us.

XV

REGRET

ONE asked of Regret,
And I made reply :

To have held the bird,
 And let it fly ;
To have seen the star
 For a moment nigh,
And lost it
 Through a slothful eye ;
To have plucked the flower
 And cast it by ;
To have one only hope—
 To die.

XVI

LOVE AFAR

Love, art thou lonely to-day ?
 Lost love that I never see,
Love that, come noon or come night,
 Comes never to me ;
Love that I used to meet
 In the hidden past, in the land
Of forbidden sweet.

Love ! do you never miss
The old light in the days ?
Does a hand

Come and touch thee at whiles
Like the wand of old smiles,
Like the breath of old bliss?
Or hast thou forgot,
And is all as if not?

What was it we swore?
    ' Evermore !
    I and Thou,'
Ah, but Fate held the pen
    And wrote N
    Just before :
    So that now,
See, it stands,
Our seals and our hands,
    ' I and Thou,
    Nevermore !'

We said ' It is best !'
And then, dear, I went
And returned not again.
Forgive that I stir,
Like a breath in thy hair,
The old pain,
'Twas unmeant.
I will strive, I will wrest
Iron peace—it *is* best.

But, O for thy hand
   Just to hold for a space,
For a moment to stand
   In the light of thy face ;
Translate Then to Now,
To hear 'Is it Thou ?'
    And reply
    'It is I !'
Then, then I could rest,
Ah, then I could wait
    Long and late.

XVII

Canst thou be true across so many miles,
   So many days that keep us still apart ?
Ah, canst thou live upon remembered smiles,
   And ask no warmer comfort for thy heart ?

I call thy name right up into the sky,
   Dear name, O surely she shall hear and hark !
Nay, though I toss it singing up so high,
   It drops again, like yon returning lark.

O be a dove, dear name, and find her breast,
   There croon and croodle all the lonely day ;
Go tell her that I love her still the best,
   So many days, so many miles, away.

POSTSCRIPT

So sang young Love in high and holy dream
  Of a white Love that hath no earthly taint,
So rapt within his vision he did seem
  Less like a boyish singer than a saint.

Ah, Boy, it is a dream for life too high,
  It is a bird that hath no feet for earth :
Strange wings, strange eyes, go seek another sky
  And find thy fellows of an equal birth.

For many a body-sweet material thing,
  What canst thou give us half so dear as these ?
We would not soar amid the stars to sing,
  Warm and content amid the nested trees.

Young Seraph, go and take thy song to heaven,
  We would not grow unhappy with our lot,
Leave us the simple love the earth hath given—
  Sing where thou wilt, so that we hear thee not.

COR CORDIUM

TO MY WIFE, MILDRED

Dear wife, there is no word in all my songs
But unto thee belongs :
Though I indeed before our true day came
Mistook thy star in many a wandering flame,
Singing to thee in many a fair disguise,
Calling to thee in many another's name,
Before I knew thine everlasting eyes.

Faces that fled me like a hunted fawn
I followed singing, deeming it was Thou,
Seeking this face that on our pillow now
Glimmers behind thy golden hair like dawn,
And, like a setting moon, within my breast
Sinks down each night to rest.

Moon follows moon before the great moon flowers.
Moon of the wild wild honey that is ours ;
Long must the tree strive up in leaf and root,
Before it bear the golden-hearted fruit :
And shall great Love at once perfected spring,
Nor grow by steps like any other thing ?

45

The lawless love that would not be denied,
The love that waited, and in waiting died,
The love that met and mated, satisfied.

Ah, love, 'twas good to climb forbidden walls,
Who would not follow where his Juliet calls ?
'Twas good to try and love the angel's way,
With starry souls untainted of the clay ;
But, best the love where earth and heaven meet,
The god made flesh and dwelling in us, sweet.

(October 22, 1891.)

THE DESTINED MAID: A PRAYER

(Chant Royal)

O MIGHTY Queen, our Lady of the fire,
    The light, the music, and the honey, all
Blent in one Power, one passionate Desire
    Man calleth Love—'Sweet love,' the blessed
        call—:
I come a sad-eyed suppliant to thy knee,
If thou hast pity, pity grant to me ;
    If thou hast bounty, here a heart I bring
    For all that bounty 'thirst and hungering.
O Lady, save thy grace, there is no way
    For me, I know, but lonely sorrowing—
Send me a maiden meet for love, I pray !

I lay in darkness, face down in the mire,
    And prayed that darkness might become my
        pall ;
The rabble rout roared round me like some quire
    Of filthy animals primordial ;

47

My heart seemed like a toad eternally
Prisoned in stone, ugly and sad as he ;
   Sweet sunlight seemed a dream, a mythic thing,
   And life some beldam's dotard gossiping.
Then, Lady, I bethought me of thy sway,
   And hoped again, rose up this prayer to wing—
Send me a maiden meet for love, I pray !

Lady, I bear no high resounding lyre
   To hymn thy glory, and thy foes appal
With thunderous splendour of my rhythmic ire ;
   A little lute I lightly touch and small
My skill thereon : yet, Lady, if it be
I ever woke ear-winning melody,
   'Twas for thy praise I sought the throbbing string,
   Thy praise alone—for all my worshipping
Is at thy shrine, thou knowest, day by day,
   Then shall it be in vain my plaint to sing ?—
Send me a maiden meet for love, I pray !

Yea ! why of all men should this sorrow dire
   Unto thy servant bitterly befall ?
For, Lady, thou dost know I ne'er did tire
   Of thy sweet sacraments and ritual ;
In morning meadows I have knelt to thee,
In noontide woodlands hearkened hushedly
   Thy heart's warm beat in sacred slumbering,

And in the spaces of the night heard ring
Thy voice in answer to the spheral lay :
    Now 'neath thy throne my suppliant life I fling—
Send me a maiden meet for love, I pray !

I ask no maid for all men to admire,
    Mere body's beauty hath in me no thrall,
And noble birth, and sumptuous attire,
    Are gauds I crave not—yet shall have withal,
With a sweet difference, in my heart's own She,
Whom words speak not but eyes know when they
    see.
    Beauty beyond all glass's mirroring,
    And dream and glory hers for garmenting ;
Her birth—O Lady, wilt thou say me nay ?—
    Of thine own womb, of thine own nurturing—
Send me a maiden meet for love, I pray !

ENVOI

Sweet Queen who sittest at the heart of spring,
My life is thine, barren or blossoming ;
    'Tis thine to flush it gold or leave it grey :
And so unto thy garment's hem I cling—
    Send me a maiden meet for love, I pray !

(*January* 13, 1888.)

D

WITH SOME OLD LOVE VERSES

Dear Heart, this is my book of boyish song,
  The changing story of the wandering quest
  That found at last its ending in thy breast—
The love it sought and sang astray so long
With wild young heart and happy eager tongue.
  Much meant it all to me to seek and sing,
  Ah, Love, but how much more to-day to bring
This 'rhyme that first of all he made when young.'

Take it and love it, 'tis the prophecy
  For whose poor silver thou hast given me gold;
    Yea! those old faces for an hour seemed fair
    Only because some hints of Thee they were:
  Judge then, if I so loved weak types of old,
How good, dear Heart, the perfect gift of Thee.

IN A COPY OF MR. SWINBURNE'S
TRISTRAM OF LYONESSE

DEAR Heart, what thing may symbolise for us
  A love like ours, what gift, whate'er it be,
  Hold more significance 'twixt thee and me
Than paltry words a truth miraculous;
Or the poor signs that in astronomy
  Tell giant splendours in their gleaming might:
  Yet love would still give such, as in delight
To mock their impotence—so this for thee.

This song for thee! our sweetest honeycomb
  Of lovesome thought and passion-hearted rhyme,
    Builded of gold and kisses and desire,
  By that wild poet who so many a time
    Our hungering lips have blessed, until a fire
Burnt speech up and the wordless hour had come.

COMFORT AT PARTING

O LITTLE Heart,
So much I see
Thy hidden smart,
So much I long
To sing some song
To comfort thee.

For, little Heart,
Indeed, indeed,
The hour to part
Makes cruel speed ;
Yet, dear, think thou
How even now,
With happy haste,
With eager feet,
The hour when we
Again shall meet
Cometh across the waste.

HAPPY LETTER

Fly, little note,
And know no rest
Till warm you lie
Within that nest
Which is her breast;
Though why to thee
Such joy should be
Who carest not,
While I must wait
Here desolate,
I cannot wot.
O what I'd do
To come with you!

PRIMROSE AND VIOLET

PRIMROSE and Violet—
May they help thee to forget
All that love should not remember,
Sweet as meadows after rain
When the sun has come again,
As woods awakened from December.
How they wash the soul from stain !
How they set the spirit free !
Take them dear, and pray for me.

'JULIET AND HER ROMEO'

(*With Mr. Dicksee's Picture*)

TAKE 'this of Juliet and her Romeo,'
    Dear Heart of mine, for though yon budding sky
Yearns o'er Verona, and so long ago
    That kiss was kissed; yet surely Thou and I,
Surely it is, whom morning tears apart,
    As ruthless men tear tendrilled ivy down:
    Is not Verona warm within thy gown,
And Mantua all the world save where thou art?

O happy grace of lovers of old time,
    Living to love like gods, and dead to live
        Symbols and saints for us who follow them;
    Even bitter Death must sweets to lovers give:
        See how they wear their tears for diadem,
Throned on the star of an unshaken rhyme.

IN HER DIARY

Go, little book, and be the looking-glass
    Of her dear soul,
The mirror of her moments as they pass,
    Keeping the whole;
Wherein she still may look on yesterday
    To-day to cheer,
And towards To-morrow pass upon her way
    Without a fear.
For yesterday hath never won a crown,
    However fair,
But that To-day a better for its own
    Might win and wear;
And yesterday hath never joyed a joy,
    However sweet,
That this To-day or that To-morrow too
    May not repeat.
Think too, To-day is trustee for to-morrow,
    And present pain
That's bravely borne shall ease the future sorrow;
    Nor cry in vain
‘Spare us To-day, To-morrow bring the rod,’
    For then again
To-morrow from To-morrow still shall borrow,
    A little ease to gain:
But bear to-day whate'er To-day may bring,
'Tis the one way to make To-morrow sing.

PARABLES

I

Dear Love, you ask if I be true,
   If other women move
The heart that only beats for you
   With pulses all of love.

Out in the chilly dew one morn
   I plucked a wild sweet rose,
A little silver bud new-born
   And longing to unclose.

I took it, loving new-born things,
   I knew my heart was warm,
'O little silver rose, come in
   And shelter from the storm.'

And soon, against my body pressed,
   I felt its petals part,
And, looking down within my breast,
   I saw its golden heart.

O such a golden heart it has,
   Your eyes may never see,
To others it is always shut,
   It opens but for me.

But that is why you see me pass
  The honeysuckle there,
And leave the lilies in the grass,
  Although they be so fair;

Why the strange orchid half-accurst—
  Circe of flowers she grows—
Can tempt me not: see! in my heart,
  Silver and gold, my rose.

II

DEEP in a hidden lane we were,
  My little love and I;
When lo! as we stood kissing there—
  A flower against the sky!

Frail as a tear its beauty hung—
  O spare it, little hand.
But innocence like its, alas!
  Desire may not withstand.

And so I clambered up the bank
  And threw the blossom down,
But we were sadder for its sake
  As we walked back to town.

A LOVE-LETTER

Darling little woman, just a little line,
  Just a little silver word
For that dear gold of thine,
  Only a whisper you have so often heard :

Only such a whisper as hidden in a shell
  Holds a little breath of all the mighty sea,
But think what a little of all its depth and swell,
  And think what a little is this little note of me.

' Darling, I love thee, that is all I live for '—
  There is the whisper stealing from the shell,
But here is the ocean, O so deep and boundless,
  And each little wave with its whisper as well.

IN THE NIGHT

' Kiss me, dear Love !'—
But there was none to hear,
   Only the darkness round about my bed
   And hollow silence, for thy face had fled,
Though in my dreaming it had come so near.

I slept again and it came back to me,
   Burning within the hollow arch of night
   Like some fair flame of sacrificial light,
And all my soul sprang up to mix with thee—
   ' Kiss me, my love !
Ah, Love, thy face how fair !'
So did I cry, but still thou wert not there.

THE CONSTANT LOVER

I SEE fair women all the day,
    They pass and pass—and go ;
I almost dream that they are shades
    Within a shadow-show.

Their beauty lays no hand on me,
    They talk—I hear no word ;
I ask my eyes if they have seen,
    My ears if they have heard.

For why—within the north countree
    A little maid, I know,
Is waiting through the days for me,
    Drear days so long and slow.

THE WONDER-CHILD

'Our little babe,' each said, 'shall be
Like unto thee'—'Like unto *thee*!'
    'Her mother's'—'Nay, his father's'—'eyes,'
    'Dear curls like thine'—but each replies,
'As thine, all thine, and nought of me.'

What sweet solemnity to see
The little life upon thy knee,
    And whisper as so soft it lies,—
      'Our little babe!'

For, whether it be he or she,
A David or a Dorothy,
    'As mother fair,' or 'father wise,'
    Both when it's 'good,' and when it cries,
One thing is certain,—it will be
      Our little babe.

MISCELLANEOUS

AN EPITHALAMIUM

SOMEWHERE safe-hidden away
   In a meadow of mortals untrod,
I saw in my dreaming to-day
   A wonderful flower of God ;
Somewhere deep buried in air,
   In a flashing abysm afar,
I came in my dreaming aware
   Of the beam of a mystical star :
And I knew that each wonderful thing
Was the song that I never may sing.

Song of a love such as rang
   Through the strings of the lyres of old,
Such song as the makers sang
   When the world was all morning and gold;
Too great for a silken time
   Fain of lutists and liers-at-ease,
Builders of honeycomb rhyme,
   Soft slaves of an opiate peace—
Such lovers were strange for these years,
Too mean for the greatness of tears.

E

Yet, might I but stretch forth my hand
   And gather that wonderful bloom,
Might I pluck and set over our land
   That star as a sign in the doom:
Then never a story of old
   Were more as a rainbow in heaven,
Were more as a water outrolled
   From a rock in the wilderness riven,
Were more as a sheltering tree,
Than this story of Her and of Thee.

O where might we look for a song,
   We lovers who faint in the way,
In a way ne'er so bitter and long
   As the thorns and the miles of your day;
We lovers who drown in the stress
   Of a sea that had made you but strong,
In the hour of our weariness,
   O where might we look for a song
Such comfort and courage to bring
As your song which I never may sing.

But vain is the breath of desire,
   And the voice of complaining is weak
To call back the soul to the lyre
   And give us the singer we seek;
High song must await the High Singer

Though we thirst through a desert of years,
And the lyre must await its Apollo,
   Though it grow all arust with our tears.
Let thy voice then no longer complain,
Thou mouth that may never attain !

So I, who were fain of your story
   To be its high-priest to the throng,
To embody its mystical glory
   In a great eucharistical song,
May know all the strength and the healing
   Of its bread and its wonderful wine,
But none other may know the revealing
   Through unsanctified singing of mine ;
Never another of me shall take
Its wine of my chalice, its bread that I break.

Yet still may it be for my glory,
   Though never the priesthood to bear,
To bend in the shrine of your story,
   As the lowliest acolyte there ;
And would that the rhyme I am bringing,
   A censer incuriously wrought,
Might seem not too poor for the swinging,
   Nor too simple the gums I have brought :
No marvel of gold-carven censer,
No frankincense fragrance or myrrh.

And O if some light from the splendour
   Of mystical Host might strike through
These wreaths as they rise and transfigure
   Their grey to a glory for you,
A glory for you as the sunrise
   Of the years that to-night have begun,
What singer would ask for his songcraft
   Boon richer than that I had won?
What token to augur were given
More bright with the blessing of Heaven!

And O that these faint-breathing spices
   Might seem for a moment as sweet
As the hearts of those roses of Isis
   To blossom at last as you meet,
Great flowers of a far-away sowing
   Of seeds that long bided the years,
In a horror of darkness safe-growing,
   Fed of ashes and suckled of tears;
Or sweet as the breath of the dawn-light
Soft flushing the fields of your love-night.

O love-night too sacred for bride-song,
   For nuptial rabble and rite,
The eyes and the tongues of a guest-throng,
   What have they to do with your night?

Your night of the Star in the Silence,
   The Rose in a trance of hushed breath,
Of God in a chariot of incense,
   And the transfiguration of Death ;
Blest guide on the travel eternal
From love unto love, ever-vernal.

Do the stars crave a priest for their wedding,
   Or the flowers of the woodland way ?
And shall man need a priestly bestedding,
   Doth he marry less sweetly than they ?
Yea, the cattle miscallèd our men-folk,
   Rank waves of a wallowing sea,
May need such a ring and a neck yoke,
   But never such lovers as ye !
Splendid as stars in their shining,
Fragrant as blossoms entwining.

But, censer, have done with thy swinging,
   With incense that groweth so pale,
And, song, make an end of thy singing
   With voice that beginneth to fail ;
No glory of sunrise is in thee,
   No fragrance as breath of the day,
But a hand-grasp of loving you may be,
   A kiss on the forehead—O may
You come as a whisper of blessing
In some pause of a happy caressing.

THE HOUSE OF VENUS

Not that Queen Venus of adulterous fame,
Whose love was lust's insatiable flame—
Not hers the house I would be singer in
Whose loose-lipped servants seek a weary sin :
But mine the Venus of that morning flood
With all the dawn's young passion in her blood,
With great blue eyes and unpressed bosom sweet.
Her would I sing, and of the shy retreat
Where Love first kissed her wondering maidenhood,
And He and She first stood, with eyes afraid,
In the most golden House that God has made.

SATIETY

THE heart of the rose—how sweet
   Its fragrance to drain,
   Till the greedy brain
   Reels and grows faint
   With the garnered scent,
Reels as a dream on its silver feet.

Sweet thus to drain—then to sleep:
   For, beware how you stay
   Till the joy pass away,
   And the jaded brain
   Seeketh fragrance in vain,
And hates what it may not reap.

HESPERIDES

Dear little Heart,
  May I whisper a prayer
For a boon ere we part,
  For a kiss—may I dare
  Say—say—where ?

'Tis a valley, dear Heart,
  With two hills soft as snow,
'Tis a garden where one,
  Only one, dear, may go,
A garden where wonderful
  Gold apples grow.

And the shade of the hills
  Is an infinite rest,
And a mouth to those apples
  May ever be pressed,
Yet their honey live on : for,
  They grow—in thy Breast.

Dear flower that standest
  Sweet sentinel there,
    May I come
    To my home ?

Understandest ?
  My *home*,
Flower ;
Our
Home !
May I dare ?

O Love ! love ! I fear,
  For the air is too sweet—
Softly, love—O my dear—
  Yea, too sweet
On a sudden to meet
  Mortal mouth !
O my sweet ! O my sweet !
  The long drouth !
And at last, dear,
  O think—
The long drink !

WHAT OF THE DARKNESS?

What of the Darkness? Is it very fair?
Are there great calms and find ye silence there?
Like soft-shut lilies all your faces glow
With some strange peace our faces never know,
With some great faith our faces never dare.
Dwells it in Darkness? Do ye find it there?

Is it a Bosom where tired heads may lie?
Is it a Mouth to kiss our weeping dry?
Is it a Hand to still the pulse's leap?
Is it a Voice that holds the runes of sleep?
Day shows us not such comfort anywhere.
Dwells it in darkness? Do ye find it there?

Out of the Day's deceiving light we call,
Day that shows man so great and God so small,
That hides the stars and magnifies the grass;
O is the Darkness too a lying glass,
Or, undistracted, do ye find truth there?
What of the Darkness? Is it very fair?

AD CIMMERIOS

(*A Prefatory Sonnet for* SANTA LUCIA, *the Misses Hodgkin's Magazine for the Blind.*)

WE, deeming day-light fair, and loving well
 Its forms and dyes, and all the motley play
 Of lives that win their colour from the day,
Are fain some wonder of it all to tell
To you that in that elder kingdom dwell
 Of Ancient Night, and thus we make assay
 Day to translate to Darkness, so to say,
To talk Cimmerian for a little spell.

Yet, as we write, may we not doubt lest ye
 Should smile on us, as once our fathers smiled,
  When we made vaunt of joys they knew no
   more ;
Knowing great dreams young eyes can never see,
 Dwelling in peace unguessed of any child—
  Will ye smile thus upon our daylight lore ?

OLD LOVE-LETTERS

You ask and I send.   It is well, yea! best:
  A lily hangs dead on its stalk, ah me!
A dream hangs dead on a life it blest.
  Shall it flaunt its death where sad eyes may see,
  In the cold dank wind of our memory?
Shall we watch it rot like an empty nest?
  Nay, send the poor ghost to Mnemosyne,
Bury these shreds and behold it shall rest.

And shall life fail if one dream be sped?
  For loss of one bloom shall the lily pass?
    Nay, bury these deep round the roots, for so
    In soil of old dreams do the new dreams grow,
  New 'Hail' is begot of the old 'Alas.'
See, here are our letters, so sweet—so dead.

AN OLD MAN'S SONG

YE are young, ye are young,
   I am old, I am old ;
And the song has been sung
   And the story been told.
Your locks are as brown
   As the mavis in May,
Your hearts are as warm
   As the sunshine to-day,
But mine white and cold
   As the snow on the brae.

And Love, like a flower,
   Is growing for you,
Hands clasping, lips meeting,
   Hearts beating so true ;
While Fame like a star
In the midnight afar
   Is flashing for you.

For you the To-come,
   But for me the Gone-by,
You are panting to live,
   I am waiting to die ;

The meadow is empty,
  No flower groweth high,
And nought but a socket
  The face of the sky.

Yea, howso we dream,
  Or how bravely we do;
The end is the same,
  Be we traitor or true :
And after the bloom
  And the passion is past,
  Death cometh at last.

DEATH IN A LONDON LODGING

' YES, Sir, she's gone at last—'twas only five minutes
    ago
We heard her sigh from her corner,--she sat in the
    kitchen, you know :
We were all just busy on breakfast, John cleaning
    the boots, and I
Had just gone into the larder—but you could have
    heard that sigh
Right up in the garret, sir, for it seemed to pass
    one by
Like a puff of wind—may be 'twas her soul, who
    knows—
And we all looked up and ran to her—just in time
    to see her head
Was sinking down on her bosom and "she's gone at
    last," I said.'

So Mrs. Pownceby, meeting on the stairs
Her second-floor lodger, me, bound citywards,
Told of her sister's death, doing her best
To match her face's colour with the news :
While I in listening made a running gloss
Beneath her speech of all she left unsaid.
As—' in the kitchen,' *rather in the way,*

Poor thing; ' busy on breakfast,' awkward time,
Indeed, for one must live and lodgers' meals,
You know, must be attended to what comes—
(Or goes, I added for her) yes! indeed.
' "She's gone at last," I said,' and better perhaps,
For what had life for her but suffering?
And then, we're only poor, sir, John and I,
And she indeed was somewhat of a strain:
O! yes, it's for the best for all of us.
And still beneath all else methought I read
' What will the lodgers think, having the dead
Within the house! how inconvenient!'

What did the lodgers think?   Well, I replied
In grief's set phrase, but ' the first floor,'
I fancy, frowned at first, as though indeed
Landladies' sisters had no right to die
And taint the air for nervous lodger folk;
Then smoothed his brow out into decency,
And said, ' how sad!' and presently inquired
The day of burial, ending with the hope
His lunch would not be late like yesterday.
The maiden-lady living near the roof
Quoted Isaiah may be, or perhaps Job—
How the Lord gives, and likewise takes away,
And how exceeding blessed is the Lord!—
For she has pious features; while downstairs

Two ' medicals '—both ' decent' lads enough—
Hearkened the story out like gentlemen,
And said the right thing—almost looked it too !
Though all the while within them laughed a sea
Of student mirth, which for full half an hour
They stifled well, but then could hold no more,
As soon their mad piano testified :
While in the kitchen dinner was toward
With hiss and bubble from the cooking stove,
And now a laugh from John ran up the stairs,
And a voice called aloud—of boiling pans.

' So soon,' reflected I, ' the waters of life
Close o'er the sunken head !'   Reflected *I*,
Not that in truth I was more pitiful
To the poor dead than those about me were,
Nay, but a trick of thinking much on Life
And Death i' the piece giveth each little strand
More deep significance—love for the whole
Must make us tender for the parts, methinks,
As in some souls the equal law holds true,
Sorrow for one makes sorrow for the world.
A fallen leaf or a dead flower indeed
Has made me just as sad, or some poor bee
Dead in the early summer—what's the odds?
Death was at ' 48,' and yet what sign ?
Who seemed to know ? who could have known that
    called ?

For not a blind was lower than its wont—
'The lodgers would not like them down,' you know—
And in all rooms, save one, the boisterous life
Blazed like the fires within the several grates—
Save one where lay the poor dead silent thing,
A closet chill as who hath sat at night
With love beside the ingle knows the ashes
In the morning.

                    Death was at '48,'
Yet Life and Love and Sunlight were there too.
I ate and slept, and morning came at length
And brought my Lady's letter to my bed :
Thrice read and thirty kisses, came a thought,
As the sweet morning laughed about the room,
Of the poor face downstairs, the sunshine there
Playing about it like a wakeful child
Whose weary mother sleepeth in the dawn,
Pressing soft fingers round about the eyes
To make them open, then with laughing shout
Making a gambol all her body's length.
Ah me ! poor eyes that never open more !
And mine as blithe to meet the morning's glance
As thirsty lips to close on thirsty lips !
Poor limbs no sun could ever warm again !
And mine so eager for the coming day !

TIME FLIES

On drives the road—another mile! and still
Time's horses gallop down the lessening hill
O why such haste, with nothing at the end!
Fain are we all, grim driver, to descend
And stretch with lingering feet the little way
That yet is ours—O stop thy horses, pray!

Yet, sister dear, if we indeed had grace
To win from Time one lasting halting-place,
Which out of all life's valleys would we choose,
And, choosing—which with willingness would lose?
Would we as children be content to stay,
Because the children are as birds all day;

Or would we still as youngling lovers kiss,
Fearing the ardours of the greater bliss?
The maid be still a maid and never know
Why mothers love their little blossoms so,
Or can the mother be content her bud
Shall never open out of babyhood?

Ah yes, Time flies because we fain would fly,
It is such ardent souls as you and I,
Greedy of living, give his wings to him—
And now we grumble that he uses them!

SO SOON TIRED!

Am I so soon grown tired?—yet this old sky
Can open still each morn so blue an eye,
This great old river still through nights and days
Run like a happy boy to holidays,
This sun be still a bridegroom, though long
    wed,
And still those stars go singing up the night,
Glad as yon lark there splashing in the light:
Are these old things indeed unwearièd,
Yet I, so soon grown tired, would creep away to
    bed!

AUTUMN

THE year grows still again, the surging wake
  Of full-sailed summer folds its furrows up,
    As after passing of an argosy
    Old Silence settles back upon the sea,
  And ocean grows as placid as a cup.
    Spring, the young morn, and Summer, the
      strong noon,
Have dreamed and done and died for Autumn's
    sake :
  Autumn that finds not for a loss so dear
    Solace in stack and garner hers too soon—
  Autumn, the faithful widow of the year.

Autumn, a poet once so full of song,
  Wise in all rhymes of blossom and of bud,
Hath lost the early magic of his tongue,
  And hath no passion in his failing blood.
Hear ye no sound of sobbing in the air ?
  'Tis his.   Low bending in a secret lane,
Late blooms of second childhood in his hair,
    He tries old magic, like a dotard mage ;
    Tries spell and spell, to weep and try again :
Yet not a daisy hears, and everywhere
    The hedgerow rattles like an empty cage.

He hath no pleasure in his silken skies,
　　Nor delicate ardours of the yellow land ;
Yea, dead, for all its gold, the woodland lies,
　　And all the throats of music filled with sand.
Neither to him across the stubble field
　　May stack nor garner any comfort bring,
　　　Who loveth more this jasmine he hath made,
　　The little tender rhyme he yet can sing,
Than yesterday, with all its pompous yield,
　　Or all its shaken laurels on his head.

A FROST FANCY

Summer gone,
Winter here ;
Ways are white,
Skies are clear.
And the sun
A ruddy boy
All day sliding,
While at night
The stars appear
Like skaters gliding
On a mere.

THE WORLD IS WIDE

THE world is wide—around yon court,
　Where dirty little children play,
Another world of street on street
　Grows wide and wider every day.

And round the town for endless miles
　A great strange land of green is spread—
O wide the world, O weary-wide,
　But it is wider overhead.

For could you mount yon glittering stairs
　And on their topmost turret stand,—
Still endless shining courts and squares,
　And lanes of lamps on every hand.

And, might you tread those starry streets
　To where those long perspectives bend,
O you would cast you down and die—
　Street upon street, world without end.

SAINT CHARLES!

'"Saint Charles," said Thackeray to me, thirty years ago, putting one of Charles Lamb's letters to his forehead.'—LETTERS OF EDWARD FITZGERALD.

SAINT CHARLES! ah yes, let other men
Love Elia for his antic pen,
And watch with dilettante eyes
His page for every quaint surprise,
Curious of *caviare* phrase.
Yea; these who will not also praise?
We surely must, but which is more
The motley that his sorrow wore,
Or the great heart whose valorous beat
Upheld his brave unfaltering feet
Along the narrow path he chose,
And followed faithful to the close?

Yea, Elia, thank thee for thy wit,
How poor our laughter, lacking it!
For all thy gillyflowers of speech
Gramercy, Elia; but most rich
Are we, most holpen, when we meet
Thee and thy Bridget in the street,
Upon that tearful errand set—
So often trod, so patient yet!

GOOD-NIGHT

(AFTER THE NORWEGIAN OF ROSENCRANTZ JOHNSEN)

MIDNIGHT, and through the blind the moonlight
    stealing
  On silver feet across the sleeping room,
Ah, moonlight, what is this thou art revealing—
  Her breast, a great sweet lily in the gloom.

It is their bed, white little isle of bliss
  In the dark wilderness of midnight sea,—
Hush! 'tis their hearts still beating from the kiss,
  The warm dark kiss that only night may see.

Their cheeks still burn, they close and nestle yet,
  Ere, with faint breath, they falter out good-night,
Her hand in his upon the coverlet
  Lies in the silver pathway of the light.

(LILLEHAMMER, *August* 22, 1892.)

NEÆRA'S HAIR

Let me take thy hair down, sweetheart,
    loosen little pin by pin,
Let me feel it tumbling o'er me
    drinking all its fragrance in,
Let me wrap thee all within it,
    kiss thee through its golden thread,—
O I shall go mad with kissing,
    kissing, kissing thy dear head.

Let me walk within this garden,
    I can smell the roses there,
They are even sweeter, darling,
    than the violets of thy hair,
Just one butterfly sweet minute,
    one deep kiss, and then away—
Unless, sweetheart, you would rather,
    rather, dear, that I should stay.

O thy body, sweet sweet body,
    let me drink and drink and drink!
Canst thou let me, like the minstrel,
    die upon the fountain's brink?
Love, O Love, what *art* Thou? tell me:
    is this heaven, hell, or where?
All I know is that I kiss thee,
    lying in thy yellow hair.

BEATRICE

(FOR THE BEATRICE CELEBRATION, 1890)

NINE mystic revolutions of the spheres
 Since Dante's birth, and lo ! a star new-born
 Shining in heaven : and like a lark at morn
Springing to meet it, straight in all men's ears,
A strange new song, which through the listening years
 Grew deep as lonely sobbing from the thorn
 Rising at eve, shot through with bitter scorn,
Full-throated with the ecstasy of tears.

Long since that star arose, that song upsprang,
 That shine and sing in heaven above us yet ;
  Since thy white childhood, glorious Beatrice,
  Dawned like a blessed angel upon his :
 Thy star it was that did his song beget,
Star shining for us still because he sang.

A CHILD'S EVENSONG

THE sun is weary, for he ran
  So far and fast to-day ;
The birds are weary, for who sang
  So many songs as they ?
The bees and butterflies at last
  Are tired out, for just think too
How many gardens through the day
  Their little wings have fluttered through.
  And so, as all tired people do,
They 've gone to lay their sleepy heads
Deep deep in warm and happy beds.
The sun has shut his golden eye
And gone to sleep beneath the sky,
The birds and butterflies and bees
Have all crept into flowers and trees,
And all lie quiet, still as mice,
Till morning comes—like father's voice.

So Geoffrey, Owen, Phyllis, you
Must sleep away till morning too.
Close little eyes, down little heads,
And sleep—sleep—sleep in happy beds.

AN EPITAPH ON A GOLDFISH

(WITH APOLOGIES TO ARIEL)

FIVE inches deep Sir Goldfish lies,
    Here last September was he laid,
Poppies these that were his eyes,
    Of fish-bones were these bluebells made.
His fins of gold that to and fro
Waved and waved so long ago,
Still as petals wave and wave
To and fro above his grave.
Hearken too ! for so his knell
Tolls all day each tiny bell.

BEAUTY ACCURST

I AM so fair that wheresoe'er I wend
  Men yearn with strange desire to kiss my face,
Stretch out their hands to touch me as I pass,
  And women follow me from place to place.

A poet writing honey of his dear
  Leaves the wet page,—ah ! leaves it long to dry.
The bride forgets it is her marriage-morn,
  The bridegroom too forgets as I go by.

Within the street where my strange feet shall stray
  All markets hush and traffickers forget,
In my gold head forget their meaner gold,
  The poor man grows unmindful of his debt.

Two lovers kissing in a secret place,
  Should I draw nigh,—will never kiss again ;
I come between the king and his desire,
  And where I am all loving else is vain.

Lo ! when I walk along the woodland way
  Strange creatures leer at me with uncouth love,
And from the grass reach upward to my breast,
  And to my mouth lean from the boughs above.

The sleepy kine move round me in desire
 And press their oozy lips upon my hair,
Toads kiss my feet and creatures of the mire,
 The snails will leave their shells to watch me
   there.

But all this worship, what is it to me?
 I smite the ox and crush the toad in death :
I only know I am so very fair,
 And that the world was made to give me breath.

I only wait the hour when God shall rise
 Up from the star where he so long hath sat,
And bow before the wonder of my eyes
 And set *me* there—I am so fair as that.

A MAID IN THE MEADOW

I

Dew in the meadow and flowers fair,
And happy songs on the morning air,
Like silver flutes the blackbirds call,
But a maid in the meadow is best of all.

'O maid, O maid, it was you they meant
With their dewy song, and shine and scent,
It was you I know that I went to meet,
But, ah! the dream was not half so sweet.'

O blackbird bold !
O blackbird old !
Shrill was your whistle of warning,
So many a maid
Have you seen betrayed
By men in the meadows at morning.

But your voice was too sweet to warn, brave bird,
It was only the music the maiden heard,
It was only your song that filled her head,
Your song and the words that the gallant said.

He had a dainty body fair
That maiden's eyes must follow after,
And O he had such bonny hair
And such a merry laughter.

She had a body like a rose,
    Her eyes were like the dew there,
Her breast a garden under snows—
    Ah! how the violets grew there!

O life is sweet, but nought so sweet
    As this in morning weather,
A man and maid with mouths that meet
    And hearts that beat together.

O life is sad, but nought so sad
    As when the sun is setting
That one forgets the joy they had,
    And one has no forgetting.

II

Frost on the meadow, no flowers fair,
No song, no light, no maiden there;
But look for her down in the village street—
'Tis she, I know, that they go to meet,
'Tis she, I know, that they walk before,
For she walks in the meadows nevermore.

O nightingale!
O nightingale!
What is the use of weeping!
So many a maid
Have you seen laid
Down there where she is sleeping.

TO A DEAD FRIEND

AND is it true indeed, and must you go,
    Set out alone across that moorland track,
No love avail, though we have loved you so,
    No voice have any power to call you back?
And losing hands stretch after you in vain,
    And all our eyes grow empty for your lack,
Nor hands, nor eyes, know aught of you again.

Dear friend, I shed no tear while yet you stayed,
    Nor vexed your soul with unavailing word,
But you are gone, and now can all be said,
    And tear and sigh too surely fall unheard.
So long I kept for you an undimmed eye,
    Surely for grief this hour may well be spared,
Though could you know I still must keep it dry.

For what can tears avail you? the spring rain
    That softly pelts the lattice, as with flowers,
Will of its tears a daisied counterpane
    Weave for your rest, and all its sound of showers
Make of its sobbing low a cradle song:
    All tears avail but these salt tears of ours,
These tears alone 'tis idle to prolong.

Yet must we shed them, barren though they be,
    Though bloom nor burden answer as they flow,
Though no sun shines that our sad eyes can see
    To throw across their fall hope's radiant bow.
Poor selfish tears! we weep them not for him,
    'Tis our own sorrow that we pity so,
'Tis our own loss that leaves our eyes so dim.

SUNSET IN THE CITY

Above the town a monstrous wheel is turning,
  With glowing spokes of red,
Low in the west its fiery axle burning ;
  And, lost amid the spaces overhead,
A vague white moth, the moon, is fluttering.

Above the town an azure sea is flowing,
  'Mid long peninsulas of shining sand,
From opal unto pearl the moon is growing,
  Dropped like a shell upon the changing strand.

Within the town the streets grow strange and
    haunted,
  And, dark against the western lakes of green,
The buildings change to temples, and unwonted
  Shadows and sounds creep in where day has been.

Within the town, the lamps of sin are flaring,
  Poor foolish men that know not what ye are !
Tired traffic still upon his feet is faring—
  Two lovers meet and kiss and watch a star.

THE CITY IN MOONLIGHT

DEAR city in the moonlight dreaming,
    How changed and lovely is your face ;
Where is the sordid busy scheming
    That filled all day the market-place ?

Was it but fancy that a rabble
    Of money-changers bought and sold,
Filling with sacrilegious babble
    This temple-court of solemn gold ?

Ah no, poor captive-slave of Crœsus,
    His bond-maid all the toiling day,
You, like some hunted child of Jesus,
    Steal out beneath the moon to pray.

OF POETS AND POETRY

INSCRIPTIONS

Poet, a truce to your song !
　　Have you heard the heart sing ?
　　　Like a brook among trees,
　　　Like the humming of bees,
　　　Like the ripple of wine :
　　Had you heard, would you stay
　　Blowing bubbles so long ?
　　You have ears for the spheres—
　　　Have you heard the heart sing ?

———

Have you loved the good books of the world,—
　　And written none ?
Have you loved the great poet,—
　　And burnt your little rhyme ?
' O be my friend, and teach me to be thine.'

———

By many hands the work of God is done,
Swart toil, pale thought, flushed dream, he
　　spurneth none :
Yea ! and the weaver of a little rhyme
Is seen his worker in his own full time.

105

THE DÉCADENT TO HIS SOUL

THE Décadent was speaking to his soul—
Poor useless thing, he said,
Why did God burden me with such as thou ?
The body were enough,
The body gives me all.

The soul's a sort of sentimental wife
That prays and whimpers of the higher life,
Objects to latch-keys, and bewails the old,
The dear old days, of passion and of dream,
When life was a blank canvas, yet untouched
Of the great painter Sin.

Yet, little soul, thou hast fine eyes,
And knowest fine airy motions,
Hast a voice—
Why wilt thou so devote them to the church ?

His face grew strangely sweet—
As when a toad smiles.
He dreamed of a new sin :
An incest 'twixt the body and the soul.

He drugged his soul, and in a house of sin
She played all she remembered out of heaven
For him to kiss and clip by.
He took a little harlot in his hands,
And she made all his veins like boiling oil,
Then that grave organ made them cool again.

Then from that day, he used his soul
As bitters to the over dulcet sins,
As olives to the fatness of the feast—
She made those dear heart-breaking ecstasies
Of minor chords amid the Phrygian lutes,
She sauced his sins with splendid memories,
Starry regrets and infinite hopes and fears;
His holy youth and his first love
Made pearly background to strange-coloured vice.

Sin is no sin when virtue is forgot.
It is so good in sin to keep in sight
The white hills whence we fell, to measure by—
To say I was so high, so white, so pure,
And am so low, so blood-stained and so base;
I revel here amid the sweet sweet mire
And yonder are the hills of morning flowers:
So high, so low; so lost and with me yet;
To stretch the octave 'twixt the dream and deed,
Ah, that's the thrill!

To dream so well, to do so ill,—
There comes the bitter-sweet that makes the sin.

First drink the stars, then grunt amid the mire,
So shall the mire have something of the stars,
And the high stars be fragrant of the mire.

The Décadent was speaking to his soul—
Dear witch, I said the body was enough.
How young, how simple as a suckling child !
And then I dreamed—'an incest 'twixt the body
    and the soul :'
Let's wed, I thought, the seraph with the dog,
And wait the purple thing that shall be born.

And now look round—seest thou this bloom ?
Seven petals and each petal seven dyes,
The stem is gilded and the root in blood :
That came of thee.
Yea, all my flowers were single save for thee.
I pluck seven fruits from off a single tree,
I pluck seven flowers from off a single stem,
I light my palace with the seven stars,
And eat strange dishes to Gregorian chants :
All thanks to thee.

But the soul wept with hollow hectic face,
Captive in that lupanar of a man.

And I who passed by heard and wept for both,—
The man was once an apple-check dear lad,
The soul was once an angel up in heaven.

O let the body be a healthy beast,
And keep the soul a singing soaring bird ;
But lure thou not the soul from out the sky
To pipe unto the body in the sty.

TO A POET

As one, the secret lover of a queen,
    Watches her move within the people's eye,
    Hears their poor chatter as she passes by,
And smiles to think of what his eyes have seen ;
The little room where love did ' shut them in,'
    The fragrant couch whereon they twain did lie,
    And rests his hand where on his heart doth die
A bruisèd daffodil of last night's sin :

So, Poet, as I read your rhyme once more
    Here where a thousand eyes may read it too,
        I smile your own sweet secret smile at those
        Who deem the outer petals of the rose
    The rose's heart—I, who through grace of you,
Have known it for my own so long before.

THE PASSIONATE READER TO HIS POET

Doth it not thrill thee, Poet,
    Dead and dust though thou art,
To feel how I press thy singing
    Close to my heart?—

Take it at night to my pillow,
    Kiss it before I sleep,
And again when the delicate morning
    Beginneth to peep?

See how I bathe thy pages
    Here in the light of the sun,
Through thy leaves, as a wind among roses,
    The breezes shall run.

Feel how I take thy poem
    And bury within it my face,
As I pressed it last night in the heart of
      a flower,
    Or deep in a dearer place.

Think, as I love thee, Poet,
    A thousand love beside,
Dear women love to press thee too
    Against a sweeter side.

Art thou not happy, Poet?
   I sometimes dream that I
For such a fragrant fame as thine
   Would gladly sing and die.

Say, wilt thou change thy glory
   For this same youth of mine?
And I will give my days i' the sun
   For that great song of thine.

MATTHEW ARNOLD

(DIED, APRIL 15, 1888)

WITHIN that wood where thine own scholar strays,
　O! Poet, thou art passed, and at its bound
　Hollow and sere we cry, yet win no sound
But the dark muttering of the forest maze
We may not tread, nor pierce with any gaze ;
　And hardly love dare whisper thou hast found
　That restful moonlit slope of pastoral ground
Set in dark dingles of the songful ways.

Gone ! they have called our shepherd from the hill;
　Passed is the sunny sadness of his song,
　　That song which sang of sight and yet was brave
　To lay the ghosts of seeing, subtly strong
　　To wean from tears and from the troughs to save;
And who shall teach us now that he is still !

H

'TENNYSON' AT THE FARM

(TO L. AND H. H.)

O you that dwell 'mid farm and fold,
  Yet keep so quick undulled a heart,
I send you here that book of gold,
  So loved so long ;
The fairest art,
  The sweetest English song.

And often in the far-off town,
  When summer sits with open door,
I 'll dream I see you set it down
  Beside the churn,
Whose round shall slacken more and more,
  Till you forget to turn.

And I shall smile that you forget,
  And Dad will scold—but never mind !
Butter is good, but better yet,
  Think such as we,
To leave the farm and fold behind,
  And follow such as he.

'THE DESK'S DRY WOOD'

(TO JAMES A. WELCH)

DEAR Desk, Farewell!   I spoke you oft
In phrases neither sweet nor soft,
But at the end I come to see
That thou a friend hast been to me,
    No flatterer but very friend.
For who shall teach so well again
The blessèd lesson-book of pain,
The truth that souls that would aspire
Must bravely face the scourge and fire,
    If they would conquer in the end?
Two days!
Shall I not hug thee very close?
Two days,
And then we part upon our ways.
Ah me!
Who shall possess thee after me?
O pray he be no enemy to poesy,
To gentle maid or gentle dream.

How have we dreamed together, I and thou,
Sweet dreams that like some incense wrapt us
        round—

The last new book, the last new love,

The last new trysting-ground.

How many queens have ruled and passed

Since first we met; how thick and fast

The letters used to come at first, how thin at
     last ;

Then ceased, and winter for a space !

Until another hand

Brought spring into the land,

And went the seasons' pace.

And now, Dear Desk, thou knowest for how long
     time

I have no queen but song :

Yea, thou hast seen the last love fade, and now

Behold the last of many a secret rhyme !

A LIBRARY IN A GARDEN

'A Library in a garden! The phrase seems to contain the whole felicity of man.'—Mr. EDMUND GOSSE in *Gossip in a Library*.

A WORLD of books amid a world of green,
Sweet song without, sweet song again within ;
Flowers in the garden, in the folios too :
O happy Bookman, let me live with you !

ON THE MORALS OF POETS

ONE says he is immoral, and points out
    Warm sin in ruddy specks upon his soul :
Bigot, one folly of the man you flout
    Is more to God than thy lean life is whole.

TO A GREAT CRITIC—ANDREW LANG, ESQ.

(WITH A VOLUME OF THE MINOR VERSE)

[Mr. Lang, writing, in 'Books and Bookmen,' of the presentation copies of 'Amateur Poets,' with which his life is made a burden, says: 'It is, no doubt, wise to turn these gifts with their sides against the inner walls of bookcases, to be bulwarks against the damp.']

My little book, I envy thee,
    For few doth Fortune favour so,
It might have been thy destiny
    Some sleepy relative to know,
    Or like proverbial lamb to go
For slaughter of some critic fang :
    But thine, secure from fool and foe—
To line the shelves of Andrew Lang.

Small is my hope, small book, that he
    For whom I write this *ex dono*
Shall feel the beating heart in thee,
    And cheer us on, my book ; ah no !
    We are presumptuous dreaming so :
Rather he 'll bid us both—go hang !
    Or even hotly bid us go
To—line the shelves of Andrew Lang.

Yet, little book, I do not see
    That such a fate need cause thee woe,
For very sweet 'twould seem to me
    To line his sweet seraglio
    Of *bouquins*, nestling row on row ;
Indeed 'twould bring no pain or pang,
    But rather set my heart aglow
To line the shelves of Andrew Lang.

O bards of unbought balladry,
    Not all in vain it was you sang,
Seems it not more than £ s. d.
    To line the shelves of—ANDREW LANG ?

FAERY GOLD

A POET hungered, as well he might—
Not a morsel since yesternight!
And sad he grew—good reason why—
For the poet had nought wherewith to buy.

'Are not two sparrows sold,' he cried,
'Sold for a farthing? and,' he sighed,
As he pushed his morning post away,
'Are not two sonnets more than they?'

Yet store of gold, great store had he,—
Of the gold that is known as 'faery.'
He had the gold of his burning dreams,
He had his golden rhymes—in reams,
He had the strings of his golden lyre,
And his own was that golden west on fire.

But the poet knew his world too well
To dream that such would buy or sell.
He had his poets, 'pure gold,' he said,
But the man at the bookstall shook his head,
And offered a grudging half-a-crown
For the five the poet had brought him down.

Ah, what a world we are in! we sigh,
Where a lunch costs more than a Keats can buy,
And even Shakespeare's hallowed line
Falls short of the requisite sum to dine.

Yet other gold had the poet got,
For see from that grey-blue Gouda pot
Three golden tulips spouting flame—
From his love, from his love, this morn, they came,
His love he loved even more than fame.

Three golden tulips thrice more fair
Than other golden tulips were—
'And yet,' he smiled as he took one up,
And feasted on its yellow cup,—
'I wonder how many eggs you'd buy!
By Bacchus, I 've half a mind to try!
'One golden bloom for one golden yolk—
Nay, on my word, sir, I mean no joke—
Gold for gold is fair dealing, sir.'
Think of the grocer gaping there!

Or the baker, if I went and said,
—'This tulip for a loaf of bread,
God's beauty for your kneaded grain;'

Or the vintner—'For this flower of mine
A flagon, pray, of yellow wine,
And you shall keep the change for gain.'

Ah me, on what a different earth
I and these fellows had our birth,
Strange that these golden things should be
For them so poor, so rich for me.'

Ended his sigh, the poet searched his shelf—
Seeking another poet to feed himself;
Then sadly went, and, full of shame and grief,
Sold his last Swinburne for a plate of beef.

Thus poets too, to fill the hungry maw,
Must eat each other—'tis the eternal law.

THE MAKING OF SONG

A POET prayed, and the answer came—
‘ Thou shalt sing, and thy song shall bring thee fame
But this must thou give for thy silver tongue
Thrice three sorrows for each new song.’

The poet was young and the world all bloom—
‘ Give me the song, let the sorrows come.’

And so it befell that his boyhood’s pain
Was thrice more bitter and thrice again,
But his tears were pearls and his sobs were song
And the solace great if the sorrow long.

Then youth with its splendid moon i’ the sky
And its wonder-maiden and love, drew nigh,
And the heart of the poet grew so glad
He forgot his song in the joy he had.
But the maiden died—then he thought to die
But his song awoke him, and up in the sky,
For each little shining tear he shed,
He set a great shining star instead—
His singing ended, his tears were dry.

Then years went by, and he took a wife,
So dear she stood him in place of life,
And, as the blossoms come to the tree,
So came a little babe to be.
But the blossom withered in springtime frost,
And the poet sang of the thing they lost—
—'But ah, my wife, had they taken thee!'

Death heard the song, and he came one night,
And the wife lay dead in the morning light.
Now, O poet, what comfort now?
Dost thou not weep for thy boyish vow?
Yea, the poet bowed his stricken head—
—'Now let me die, for my life is dead.'

Yet, as days wore on, little leaf by leaf
Budded once more on the tree of grief,
And note by note the accustomed song
Rose, as of old, more deep, more strong;
Though something told to the listening ears
That it bubbled up from a fount of tears.

One more sorrow remained untried:
God took back his song—*then* the poet died.

ALL SUNG

WHAT shall I sing when all is sung,
  And every tale is told,
And in the world is nothing young
  That was not long since old?

Why should I fret unwilling ears
  With old things sung anew,
While voices from the old dead years
  Still go on singing too?

A dead man singing of his maid
  Makes all my rhymes in vain,
Yet his poor lips must fade and fade,
  And mine shall kiss again.

Why should I strive through weary moons
  To make my music true?
Only the dead men knew the tunes
  The live world dances to.

CORYDON'S FAREWELL TO HIS PIPE

YEA, it is best, dear friends, who have so oft
Fed full my ears with praises sweet and soft,
Sweeter and softer than my song should win,
Too sweet and soft—I must not listen more,
Lest its dear perilous honey make me mad,
And once again an overweening lad
Presume against Apollo.   Nay, no more !
'Tis not to pipes like mine sing stars at morn,
Nor stars at night dance in their solemn dance :
Nay, stars ! why tell of stars ? the very thrush
Putteth my daintiest cunning to the blush
And boasteth him the hedgerow laureate.
Yea, dimmest daisies lost amid the grass,
One might have deemed blessed us for looking at,
Would rather choose,—yea, so it is, alas !—
The meanest bird that from its tiny throat
Droppeth the pearl of one monotonous note,
Than any music I can bring to pass.

So, let me go : for, while I linger here,
Piping these dainty ditties for your ear,
To win that dearer honey for my own,
Daylong my Thestylis doth sit alone,

Weeping, mayhap, because the gods have given
Song but not sheep—the rarer gift of heaven ;
And little Phyllis solitary grows,
And little Corydon unheeded goes.

Sheep are the shepherd's business,—let me go,—
Piping his pastime when the sun is low :
But I, alas ! the other order keep,
Piping my business, and forgot my sheep.

My song that once was as a little sweet
Savouring the daily bread we all must eat,
Lo ! it has come to be my only food :
And, as a lover of the Indian weed
Steals to a self-indulgent solitude,
To draw the dreamy sweetness from its root,
So from the strong blithe world of valorous deed
I steal away to suck this singing weed ;
And while the morning gathers up its strength,
And while the noonday runneth on in might,
Until the shadows and the evening light
Come and awake me with a fear at length,
Prone in some hankering covert hid away,
Fain am I still my piping to prolong,
And for the largess of a bounteous day
Dare pay my maker with a paltry song.

Welcome the song that like a trumpet high
Lifts the tired head of battle with its cry,
Welcome the song that from its morning heights
Cheers jaded markets with the health of fields,
Brings down the stars to mock the city lights,
Or up to heaven a shining ladder builds.
But not to me belongeth such a grace,
And, were it mine, 'tis not in amorous shade
To river music that such song is made :
The song that moves the battle on awoke
To the stern rhythm of the swordsman's stroke,
The song that fans the city's weary face
Sprang not afar from out some leafy place,
But bubbled spring-like in its dingiest lane
From out a heart that shared the city's pain;
And he who brings the stars into the street
And builds that shining ladder for our feet,
Dwells in no mystic Abora aloof,
But shares the shelter of the common roof;
He learns great metres from the thunderous hum,
And all his songs pulse to the human beat.

But I am Corydon, I am not he,
Though I no more that Corydon shall be
To make a sugared comfit of my song.
So now I go, go back to Thestylis—
How her poor eyes will laugh again for this !—

Go back to Thestylis, and no more roam
In melancholy meadows mad to sing,
But teach our little home itself to sing.
Yea, Corydon, now cast thy pipe away—
See, how it floats upon the stream, and see
There it has gone, and now—away ! away !
But O ! my pipe, how sweet thou wert to me !

The writer begs to acknowledge the kind permission of the Editors of 'Macmillan's Magazine,' 'Black and White,' 'The Library,' 'The Speaker,' 'The Academy,' 'The Art Review,' for several reprints. He has also to thank Messrs. Cope for a similar permission in regard to the lines on Lamb, originally written as a proem for their Lamb 'Booklet.'

Edinburgh : T. and A. CONSTABLE

Printers to Her Majesty

THE BODLEY HEAD,
VIGO STREET, LONDON, W.,
October 1892.

Books by Richard Le Gallienne

'*Mr. Le Gallienne shares with Mr. Robert Bridges the distinction, among minor poets, of having his first editions collected by amateurs in this country and America.*'
DAILY CHRONICLE.

My Ladies' Sonnets

AND OTHER 'VAIN AMATORIOUS' VERSES

WITH SOME OF GRAVER MOOD

Privately Printed, 1887.

[*Out of print and very rare.*

Volumes in Folio

Printed at the Chiswick Press, in two Editions. 250 copies Royal 16mo, and 50 copies Large Paper, Fcap. 4to. 1889.

[*Out of print and very rare.*

LONDON: ELKIN MATHEWS AND JOHN LANE, VIGO STREET, W.

Second Edition, Crown 8vo, cloth, 7s. 6d.

George Meredith : Some Characteristics.

By RICHARD LE GALLIENNE.   With a Bibliography (much
enlarged) by JOHN LANE : Portrait, and Illustration of the
novelist's *Chalet*.   1890.

All Meredithians must possess *George Meredith: Some Characteristics*,
by Richard Le Gallienne.   This book is a complete and excellent guide to
the novelist and the novels,—a sort of Meredithian *Bradshaw*, with pictures
of the traffic superintendent, and of the head office at Boxhill.   Even Phili-
stines may be won over by the blandishments of Mr. Le Gallienne, from
whom I learn, by the way, that George Meredith is 'the Harvey of the
Ego,' and that he is not Adrian Harley.   I hear, also, that 'daily, from
one quarter or another, come critical cuff and kick, to impress upon a numb
public the latest example of its immemorial purblindness.'   And the Baron
adds this cufflet to the rest.   Mr. John Lane has added a Bibliography,
which is a model of minute industry.   So here's to the book of Richard and
John.   'The Baron de Book Worms' in PUNCH.

A very interesting and helpful book, likely to be agreeable to Mr.
Meredith's instructed admirers, and suggestive to many by whom his works
are misunderstood . . . as appreciations merely, the essays are of a high
order of literary merit.   The author's style has, indeed, been compared
with Mr. Meredith's own.   But that is a criticism which in effect is unjust,
as it suggests the difficulties of Mr. Meredith's style rather than its merits.
Occasionally Mr. Le Gallienne lays himself open to the charge of being
fantastic . . . but his style is not obscure.   It is an eager, sensitive, and
highly-figured style, somewhat of the aphoristic type.   Much of what Mr.
Le Gallienne says is admirable, for its own sake, and so far as his subject is
concerned . . . he is no unworthy guide . . . The remarks on Meredith's
idea of comedy . . . will be particularly useful to many. . . . This critic
lays no less stress on his poetry, especially on 'Modern Love.'   With the
exception of the latter, he surely overrates this part of Mr. Meredith's work.
The chapter, however, in which he discusses this is an interesting piece of
criticism, written with the fervour of an enthusiast ; yet not undiscriminat-
ing.   And the concluding sentences are a striking example of his figurative
style.   The Bibliography compiled by Mr. Lane should be very useful.
                                                              VANITY FAIR.

LONDON : ELKIN MATHEWS AND JOHN LANE, VIGO STREET, W.

Even in these days, when it is the doom of genius that thousands shall read about a man's books for one who shall read the books themselves, few of the dead and none of the living have been discussed, analysed, appreciated, with the keenness of perception, the sympathetic receptivity, the sensitive warmth, 'the love according to knowledge,' and the adequacy of expression which distinguish this generous volume of characteristics.' Mr. Le Gallienne has, with almost microscopic insight, analysed the style and aim, the intention and the methods, of one of the most powerful intellects, and certainly the most original of our time.   GLASGOW HERALD.

The Student and the Body Snatcher

AND OTHER TRIFLES.

By ROBINSON K. LEATHER, M.A., and RICHARD LE GALLIENNE. Royal 18mo, 3s. 6d. nett.   1890.

[*A few remain.*

⁎ Fifty copies on Large Paper, 7s. 6d. nett.

Second Edition, Crown 8vo, buckram, gilt top, 5s.

The Book-bills of Narcissus

AN ACCOUNT RENDERED BY RICHARD LE GALLIENNE. 1891.

With all its digressions and appeals to the gentle reader, his book is a study of character, a study of the spiritual growth and evolution of a poetic young gentleman whose many charms proved irresistible with certain booksellers and other young persons. The portraiture is delicately wrought. The pleasant touches of humour or pathos, the little strokes of irony, are so blended that you cannot detect any positive evidence of moral judgment, even when censure may seem to be implied. The whole record, in short, is harmonised, and artist and work are as one. The deliberate quaintness of style, as of a new Euphues, or a Euphues with something of the poetic grace of the old and a manner that is his own, is in perfect agreement with the theme. . . . Mr. Le Gallienne has achieved the end he had in view. He has made the 'rose of Narcissus to bloom anew.'
        SATURDAY REVIEW, Article : 'Narcissus Poeticus,' Oct. 10, 1891.

LONDON: ELKIN MATHEWS AND JOHN LANE, VIGO STREET, W.

4

If an unusually fine literary instinct could make a solid book, Mr. Le
Gallienne would be at no loss for an enduring reputation. . . . Nothing
can be prettier than his pleas and persuasions on behalf of Narcissus and
George Muncaster. . . .

'C. di B.' (Mr. Bernard Shaw) in THE STAR, Sept. 12, 1891.

The Narcissus, about whose life . . . we here learn a good deal, must
have been an agreeable companion. . . . His wayward moods, his innocent
love affairs, his wanderings, his readings, his culminating grand passion,
Mr. Le Gallienne renders his account of them all, and does it in a fresh
and breezy style which suits his pleasant subject admirably. There is a
special charm, too, about the graceful lyrics which sparkle here and there
in the pretty little volume. In fact, Mr. Le Gallienne is an artist. . . .

'The Baron's Assistant Reader,' PUNCH, Sept. 19, 1891.

Among the depressing brutalities which, on the one hand, are saluted as
the outpourings of unparalleled genius, and the Cockney vulgarities which,
on the other, are accepted as humour fit for innumerable editions, it is
pleasant to come upon a booklet so delicate, so artistic, and so fanciful as
'The Book-bills of Narcissus.' . . . I quote the delightful songs which
George Muncaster sings to his children. . . . Happy Geoffrey, Owen, and
Phyllis, say I, to have such songs to wake them and lull them to sleep!

'R. C. L.' in ILLUSTRATED LONDON NEWS, Sept. 26, 1891.

To have read a book through once delightedly and then to commence it
again is surely a test, be the reader who he may, of its interest, if not of its
worth. . . . The book is so good that it is too short.

REVIEW OF REVIEWS (with Portrait), Oct. 15, 1891.

'The Book-bills of Narcissus' was also the third in a list of six of the
popular books of the month in THE BOOKMAN for October; Mr. Kipling's
'Life's Handicap' and Mr. Besant's 'Armorel of Lyonesse' being the two
preceding.

. . . he writes with ease and enjoys the dropping of the words, the dis-
tillation of the honey as it must seem to him, and occasionally he lights the
page with a fine perception of what makes gentle and lovely character . . .
a singular little confession, a very modern one, infantile modern; but, above
all other things, it has frankness like that of youthful unconcern, only dimly
beginning to guess its own comedy.

THE NEW YORK NATION, 17th March 1892.

I wish I had space to tell you of the exquisite pages of 'The Book-bills
of Narcissus,' one of the swift successes of the London autumn . . . I should
have thought the book too subtle, too delicate, too poetic, to have caught

LONDON : ELKIN MATHEWS AND JOHN LANE, VIGO STREET, W.

so suddenly the public ear . . . you must read the book, those of you who love what is loveliest, and you will know of what a poet's heart is made.

MRS. L. CHANDLER MOULTON in THE BOSTON HERALD, Dec. 20, 1891.

. . . the book is charmingly written, with a grace and flexibility of style almost French, and a delicacy of touch very rarely to be found in modern English literature. THE NEW YORK TRIBUNE.

The Book of the Rhymers' Club.

Contributions by ERNEST DOWSON, EDWIN J. ELLIS, G. A. GREENE, LIONEL JOHNSON, RICHARD LE GALLIENNE, VICTOR PLARR, ERNEST RADFORD, ERNEST RHYS, T. W. ROLLESTON, ARTHUR SYMONS, JOHN TODHUNTER, W. B. YEATS.

Edition limited to 450 copies, 16mo [*all sold*], and 50 Large Paper Copies at 10s. 6d. nett. [*A few remain.*

The 'Rhymers' Club' is one little book of the work of twelve very competent verse writers, many of them not unknown to fame—*viz.*, to employ alphabetical order, Messrs. Dowson, Ellis, Greene, Johnson, Le Gallienne, Victor Plarr, Ernest Radford, Ernest Rhys, Rolleston, Arthur Symons, J. Todhunter, and W. B. Yeats. This form of publication is not a new departure exactly, but it is a recurrence to the excellent fashion of the Elizabethan age when 'England's Helicon,' Davidson's 'Poetical Rhapsody' and 'Phœnix Nest,' with scores of other collections, contained the best songs of the best song writers of that tuneful epoch. Here is an 'idle song' ('What of the Darkness?') of Mr. Le Gallienne, which 'the world had wanted' perhaps but for the Rhymers' Club. It is very welcome, come how it will, as the little book which contains it is welcome also.

BLACK AND WHITE.

. . . leur volume contient des choses absolument remarquables, et parmi elles, au premier rang, la très belle *Beauté maudite*, de M. Richard le Gallienne :—. . . J'ai cité de préférence la *mieux portante* de ces poésies, les autres ne m'ont paru avoir ni l'étrangeté ni la robustesse de celle-là . . .

REVUE DES REVUES.

LONDON: ELKIN MATHEWS AND JOHN LANE, VIGO STREET, W.

LIBER AMORIS;
OR, THE NEW PYGMALION

By WILLIAM HAZLITT. With an Introduction by RICHARD
  LE GALLIENNE, with the beautiful Vignette of the
  Madonna finely reproduced. Printed in Two Editions at
  the Rugby Press. 500 copies Fcap. 8vo, 5s. nett, and 50
  copies Large Paper, Post 8vo, 12s. 6d. nett.

[In preparation.

Messrs. Elkin Mathews and John Lane will shortly issue, in
a limited edition, William Hazlitt's rare LIBER AMORIS. Mr.
Le Gallienne will provide an introduction. Readers of Mr.
Le Gallienne's pretty BOOK-BILLS OF NARCISSUS will remember that Narcissus was an expert in love. The same
publishers are deferring publication of Mr. Le Gallienne's new
book of ENGLISH POEMS until the autumn. We understand
that the whole of the large-paper and the greater part of the
small-paper edition of Mr. Le Gallienne's book have already
been bought up. Mr. Le Gallienne is a very fortunate poet.
Mr. Traill must congratulate himself that he put him on his
list in time. ST. JAMES'S GAZETTE, June 25, 1892.

. . . A new edition of that rare and delectable little volume
of William Hazlitt's the LIBER AMORIS (is promised) with an
introductory chapter from the pen of Mr. Richard Le Gallienne.
It is understood that Mr. Le Gallienne's foreword is extremely
sympathetic; nay, it may almost be dubbed a defence, or
supplement. That fascinating chapter, *The Thirteenth Maid,*

LONDON: ELKIN MATHEWS AND JOHN LANE, VIGO STREET, W.

in THE BOOK-BILLS OF NARCISSUS inclines one to hope that
its author may have some interesting confessions to make
regarding one, at least, of the round dozen—be she another
'Hesper' or Eliza matters not—provided only he be frank.

DAILY CHRONICLE, June 17, 1892.

ARTHUR HALLAM
AND LORD TENNYSON

ON SOME OF THE CHARACTERISTICS OF MODERN POETRY,

AND ON THE LYRICAL POEMS OF ALFRED TENNYSON.

A review contributed to THE ENGLISHMAN'S MAGAZINE, in
the year 1831, by A. H. HALLAM. Reprinted, with an
introductory note by RICHARD LE GALLIENNE. Small
8vo. 3s. 6d. nett.

This essay, apart from its great interest as a memorial of the
friendship between Hallam and Lord Tennyson, is remarkable
for the singularly modern note of its criticism.

[In preparation.

LONDON: ELKIN MATHEWS AND JOHN LANE, VIGO STREET, W.

www.ingramcontent.com/pod-product-compliance
Lightning Source LLC
Chambersburg PA
CBHW030903050726
47500CB00009B/1000